CHRIS WORMELL

Blue Rabbit

and Friends

A Tom Maschler Book
Jonathan Cape
London

Once there was a Blue Rabbit who lived in a cave in the middle of a dark forest.

Blue Rabbit didn't like his home; the cave was too large and the forest was too dark.
So he set off to find somewhere better to live.

At the edge of the forest he found a bear sitting in a pool of water.

'Good morning, Bear,' said Blue Rabbit.

'Good morning, Blue Rabbit,' said Bear.

'I'm looking for a new home. Do you know of a good place to live?' asked Blue Rabbit.

'You can have this pool if you like,' said Bear. 'I find it rather wet.'
Blue Rabbit dipped his foot in the pool.
'Thank you, Bear, but I think I'll go on looking,' he said.
'I'll come along with you if I may,' said Bear, shaking off the drips.

Blue Rabbit and Bear came to a kennel. In the kennel lived a goose called Rover.

'Good morning, Rover,' said Blue Rabbit and Bear.

'Good morning to you both,' said Goose.

'I'm looking for a new home and so is Bear,' said Blue Rabbit. 'Do you know of a good place to live?'

'You're welcome to this kennel if you want it,' replied Goose. 'It's too dry and stuffy for me and it smells of old bones. And I don't like the name Rover.'

'I'd like somewhere dry,' said Bear peering into the kennel. 'But I don't think I'd fit in here.' Blue Rabbit sniffed inside. 'Thank you, Goose, but I'll keep on looking,' he said.

'I'll join you if I may,' replied Goose waddling after Blue Rabbit and Bear.

Further on they came to a hole in a bank. The bank was covered in daisies and in the hole lived a dog. 'Good morning, Dog,' said Blue Rabbit, Bear and Goose. 'Good morning to you all,' said Dog. 'I'm looking for a new home and so are Bear and Goose,' said Blue Rabbit. 'Do you know of a good place to live?'

'I'd like a new home, too,' said Dog. 'This hole is so cramped and I don't much care for daisies. What I want is a warm dry kennel.'

'A kennel!' cried Blue Rabbit.
'Why Goose has a kennel
–perhaps you can have that?'
'You're welcome, Dog,' said Goose.
'You might like the smell of old bones.'

They went back to Goose's kennel and Dog loved it and he liked the name Rover too.

'But what about you?' he asked Goose. 'Where will you live now?'

'What I would really like,' said Goose, 'is a nice wet pool.'

'A pool!' cried Blue Rabbit. 'Why Bear has a pool – you could have that.'

'You're welcome,' said Bear. 'It's as wet as you could wish for.'

They went back to Bear's pool and Goose loved it and splashed about happily.

'But what about you, Bear, where will you live now?' asked Goose.

'What I really want,' said Bear, 'is a snug cave in the middle of a dark forest.'

'A cave!' cried Blue Rabbit. 'I have a cave, Bear, and it's right in the middle of the forest. You can have that.'

They went back to Blue Rabbit's cave and Bear loved it and he thought the dark forest was perfect. 'But what about you, Blue Rabbit, where will you live now?' asked Bear. 'I think what I really want,' said Blue Rabbit,

'.....is adventure.'

And hopping on his bike he went off to see the world — with the open sky above and the wind in his face. 'I'll just keep looking,' he called back over his shoulder.

For Mary, Jack, Daisy & Eliza

First published 1999
1 3 5 7 9 10 8 6 4 2

First published in the United Kingdom in 1999 by
Jonathan Cape Ltd, Random House
20 Vauxhall Bridge Road, London SW1V 2SA

A CIP catalogue record for this book
is available from the British Library

ISBN 0-224-04724-8

Printed in Hong Kong by Midas Printing Limited